Sports Illustrated KIDS

ALL ACCESS

THE WAITING IS THE HARDEST PART

Knock, Knock
This door gets you behind the Green Monster, the famous leftfield wall in Boston's Fenway Park.

Getting Ready for the Show

These pieces of wood, stamped with their weight in ounces, will become big league bats.

Managing Editor, Sports Illustrated Kids **Bob Der**

Designer **Beth Bugler**

Project Editor **Andrea Woo**

Photo Editor **Marguerite Schropp-Lucarelli**

Assistant Photo Editor **Annmarie Modugno-Avila**

Editors **Justin Tejada, Sachin Shenolikar**

Writers **Aimee Crawford, Sarah Braunstein, Gary Gramling, Duane Munn, Paul Ulane**

Photo Imaging **Geoffrey Michaud, Dan Larkin, Robert Thompson, News and Business Imaging Group**

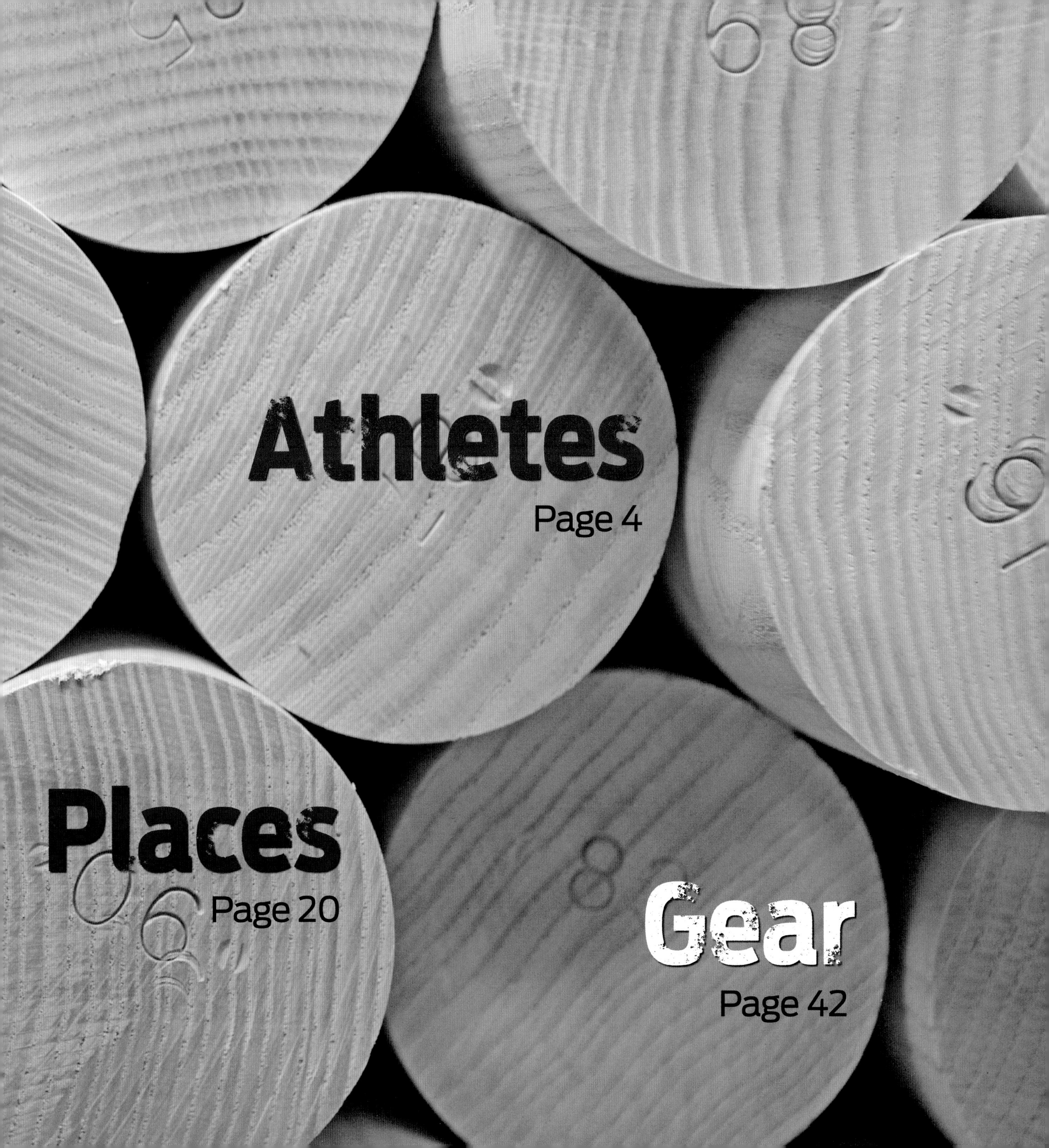

Athlete

High Five!

See how your hands measure up

"All you have to do is look at a gymnast's hands to know how much they get used. We use them in every event. I don't think the size of my hands matters much, but using them for pushing, pulling, and balancing does mean a lot."

Check out Shawn's hand!

SHAWN JOHNSON
Gymnast

HEIGHT: 4' 9"

Pet Projects

From creepy crawlers to furry rascals, these sports stars have some exotic best friends

Snapping Turtle One of Sims's newest pets is an American snapping turtle. "I'm going to keep him in my bedroom, I like him that much," says Sims.

Tarantula Sims got his first tarantula when he was 10 years old. One day, he came home to find his spider's cage was empty. "I eventually found [the spider] on my wall," Sims says. "But after that, my mom never came in my room again."

Kinkajou Sims is a proud owner of a kinkajou, a rainforest mammal known as the honey bear because it licks honey directly out of beehives. Sims's kinkajou is named Sidney.

ERNIE SIMS
Linebacker, Philadelphia Eagles

Ernie Sims dreams of opening a zoo one day. Visit
the Philadelphia Eagles linebacker's house, and
you'd think he already has one. Sims has dozens of pets,
and many of them aren't cute and cuddly. Although he has
traditional animals like dogs (Sims enters his American pit
bull terriers in dog shows), he also has a soft spot for
reptiles. Among the creatures housed in Sims's reptile
room are large snakes (including two albino Burmese
pythons), iguanas, bearded lizards, and alligators.
"Growing up, I would always play outside and just collect
[different reptiles], lizards, turtles, snakes," says Sims,
who was an environmental studies major at Florida State
University. "It was great when it rained, because the
bullfrogs would come out. Ever since
then I always loved them." Sims
often invites friends and their
families over to see his collection
and sometimes lets the pets out of
their cages to roam around. And
Sims's animal kingdom is still growing. "My parents know
not to take me to a pet store," he says. "Because if I go into
a pet store, I have to get something."

> **Owns dozens
> of reptiles**

Owns two ferrets

VISANTHE SHIANCOE
Tight End, Minnesota Vikings

Minnesota Vikings tight end Visanthe Shiancoe talks about his pet ferrets the same way opposing coaches talk about *him*. "You've always got to keep an eye on them," says Shiancoe, who led Minnesota with 11 touchdown catches in 2009. Shiancoe has large, three-story cages for his ferrets, Smoke and Gee, but he likes to let them out to run around the house and play. So are they well-behaved? "It depends on how you define *well-behaved*," Shiancoe says. "They're not going to bite anyone, but they run and jump and hop. I'll turn around for a second and then there will be a big bang and a trash can will be knocked over. Or if they see potted plants, they'll just start digging and digging until there's dirt all over the place." Usually Smoke and Gee stay at home during the season and Shiancoe's mother looks after them. But he's considering taking them on the road. Then his teammates might see why Shiancoe gets along with his ferrets so well. "They're hyperactive, always twisting and turning," he says. "Kind of like me."

PATRICK DENEEN
Freestyle Skier

Freestyle skier Patrick Deneen and his family are self-described horse people, but horses aren't the only animals that populate their farm in Cle Elum, Washington. They also have four border collie dogs, a donkey named Mr. Don Key, and two miniature donkeys named Carlos and Shawnie. "My parents went to a horse auction awhile back, and my dad saw a miniature donkey," says Deneen, the 2009 freestyle skiing world champion. "My mom didn't really want one, but when she wasn't looking, he went over and bid on a donkey and got it for $25." Carlos and Shawnie aren't yet strong enough to do much heavy lifting around the family ranch, but Deneen has big plans for them once they're older. "We want to get them hooked up to a cart," he says. "They could pull like two or three people." When Deneen isn't training or competing, he loves spending time with the animals. "When I'm home, I try to ride my horse a couple hours a day," he says. "It's a cool feeling."

Owns 26 horses, four dogs, three donkeys

Owns 300 longhorn cattle

ROSS OHLENDORF
Pitcher, Pittsburgh Pirates

Every time Pittsburgh Pirates pitcher Ross Ohlendorf takes the mound, he faces the top hitters in the major leagues. But at home he deals with even more imposing characters. Ohlendorf and his family run a cattle ranch in Lockhart, Texas, that is currently home to about 300 longhorn cattle. The cows are bred and sold to other farms, but some have been with the family so long that they're more like pets. "We still have one of the first three that we bought," says Ohlendorf. "We've had her for 15 years. Her name is Marina. She would be the most difficult for me to part with." During the off-season Ohlendorf names the calves, helps ween them from their mothers, and puts pictures of the cows on the farm's website. Luckily, there is one job he gets to avoid. "I don't have to clean up after them," he says. "They're not in stalls. They're all out in pasture."

Food For Thought

NBA great Grant Hill opens up his fridge to reveal how he and his family eat

GRANT HILL
Forward, Phoenix Suns

When Grant Hill was a kid, he never ate fruit or vegetables, and he'd drink soda on a daily basis. Even 10 years ago, a photo of his fridge would have revealed a lot of junk food. But the basketball star has grown to realize the importance of eating healthy — and he has even learned to enjoy it. "My taste buds have changed," says Hill, who will have a big fruit plate for lunch and sticks to a simple meal of fish and sweet potatoes before a game. "Maybe as an athlete I'm more sensitive to how my body feels, but I stay away from fried foods and sugary drinks."

During the week, Hill and his family are lucky to have a macrobiotic chef, who cooks meals with whole grains and beans, and does not use artificial or processed ingredients. The heathy diet has paid off for the NBA veteran. "For my performance on the court, it's necessary to eat the right kind of foods," says Hill, whose career scoring average is more than 17 points per game. "I still feel great and can run around and play — and keep up with my two daughters."

Board Meeting

Olympic gold medalist Hannah Teter shows us the snowboards that help her boost big airs

Teter has been riding the Burton Feelgood model for the past five years. She rode this 152-centimeter board in the Grand Prix qualifiers leading up to the 2010 Olympics. "It was a high-performance year, and I needed a board that was going to go for the gold with me," Teter says.

Teter offers her input each season on how boards, like this 2010 Feelgood, should ride and what the graphics should look like. "Any vision you have can be put on a snowboard," Teter says. "Different materials, all the colors of the rainbow — there's no limit."

Teter used this 2008 Burton Custom for a contest in Australia after she had broken her primary board. When she is competing, Teter travels with three snowboards, all primed and ready, so that she can quickly hop on a backup if necessary.

"That's the golden board," Teter says of the Burton Feelgood she rode to victory at the 2006 Olympics. This snowboard usually lives at her father's house in Vermont along with the one she rode at the 2010 Games.

HANNAH TETER
Snowboarder

Hannah Teter, who won the gold medal in women's halfpipe at the 2006 Winter Olympics and the silver medal in the same event at the 2010 Games, has been on some pretty smooth rides over the years. Sponsored by Burton, she gets to try out the company's boards before they are available to the public. Teter's success on those boards has also allowed her to give back. The Vermont native produces Hannah's Gold maple syrup and uses its profits to help a village in the African country of Kenya. Teter is still amazed at how far snowboarding has come. "I remember strapping in with my big Sorel [snow] boots," she says. "Now you can have the most comfy gear that performs like no other. It's come so far, so quickly."

When Teter is able to ride powder, she likes to use this Burton Malolo. The shape allows her to maneuver a smaller board in deep snow comfortably. The Sierra-at-Tahoe resort in Lake Tahoe, California, is just 10 minutes from Teter's house and serves as a great testing ground for the Malolo. "I just cruise up there and go in the trees and find my Zen zone," she says.

Kicking It

Chris Paul shows us
how his signature
sneaker was designed

Kicking It

Chris Paul shows us
how his signature
sneaker was designed

HANNAH TETER
Snowboarder

Hannah Teter, who won the gold medal in women's halfpipe at the 2006 Winter Olympics and the silver medal in the same event at the 2010 Games, has been on some pretty smooth rides over the years. Sponsored by Burton, she gets to try out the company's boards before they are available to the public. Teter's success on those boards has also allowed her to give back. The Vermont native produces Hannah's Gold maple syrup and uses its profits to help a village in the African country of Kenya. Teter is still amazed at how far snowboarding has come. "I remember strapping in with my big Sorel [snow] boots," she says. "Now you can have the most comfy gear that performs like no other. It's come so far, so quickly."

When Teter is able to ride powder, she like Burton Malolo. The shape allows her to m smaller board in deep snow comfortably. Tahoe resort in Lake Tahoe, California, is j from Teter's house and serves as a great t for the Malolo. "I just cruise up there and and find my Zen zone," she says.

STEP #3 ⤶

FINISHED!

When it came time to apply the final touches, Paul looked to his family for inspiration. For the CP3.III, five family crests appear on the sides of the sneaker. "I always try to incorporate family into everything I do," says Paul. "Now, when I wear these, it's like my family is with me on the court."

THE MEANING OF THE SYMBOLS

CJ PAUL (BROTHER)
Chris and CJ played organized basketball together for all of 15 seconds, which is why 15 appears on CJ's crest.

ROBIN PAUL (MOTHER)
The two fleurs-de-lis symbols on either side of Robin's initials are for her two sons.

PAPA CHILLY (GRANDFATHER)
The number 61 stands for the age of Paul's grandfather when he passed away and for the number of points Paul scored during a high school game in his memory.

CHARLES PAUL (FATHER)
At the time the shoe was launched, Charles and Robin had been married 28 years, so the number was incorporated into the crest.

CHRIS PAUL
The military stripes reflect Paul's role as the floor general of the New Orleans Hornets.

Places

>> TAKE AN ALL-ACCESS TOUR OF THE BEST LOCKER ROOMS AND PLACES IN SPORTS

In the House

The New York Mets' first-class facilities are simply amazin'

PLACE:	New York Mets Clubhouse
LOCATION:	Citi Field, Queens, New York
SIZE:	30,000 square feet

THE COOL STUFF:

- Players' lounge with pinball machines and a pool table
- Private chefs and a candy room
- High-tech training room with whirlpools

‹‹ Rack 'Em Up!

The players' lounge includes a large screen TV (equipped with an Xbox and *Rock Band*), pinball machines, and a pool table. But the players are reminded that there's work to be done. Hanging on the walls are the jerseys of Mets greats, such as Tom Seaver, Willie Mays, and Nolan Ryan.

>> Batter Up!

One of the biggest rooms in the clubhouse is the equipment room, which holds, among other gear, balls and bats. Each player's bat supply is labeled by jersey number, so if a bat is needed during a game, it is easy to grab. Each Met has about a dozen spare bats readily available.

<< Jersey Boys

Besides bats, jackets, sweatshirts, and hats, the equipment room also houses racks and racks of jerseys. Did you know that the average player uses about four or five uniforms in a season? Clubhouse workers hang the correct uniform and warmup gear in each player's locker before games. The Mets even keep youth-sized replica jerseys on hand for the players' kids.

<< Food and Fun

The Mets have two private chefs who cook for the team. They can prepare just about anything to order on the clubhouse grill, such as chicken, pasta, burgers, and hot dogs. While the team might prefer that the players grab an energy bar or a protein shake, there's also plenty of junk food on hand. They stock just about every kind of candy you can imagine. Players can also get a cup of coffee or an ice cream cone.

<< Water Works

In the training room, the Mets have a hydrotherapy pool. Players run under water in the pool, which takes pressure off their joints and helps hamstrings heal faster. The room also contains two hot tubs, where team members go to rest their tired muscles after a tough game.

>> Fan Favorites

The players have their own mailboxes, where fan mail is delivered each day. The bigger stars – such as centerfielder Carlos Beltran, third baseman David Wright, and pitcher Francisco Rodriguez – get larger boxes to handle all the mail they receive. Wright is so popular that he gets more letters from fans than every other Mets player combined.

Command Center on the Move

An X-ray look into the transporter for Kyle Busch's NASCAR Sprint Cup racing team

Going Places

The NASCAR team hauler — a truck used to transport the race cars from one track to another — is like a garage on wheels. The 18-wheel tractor-trailer for Kyle Busch's team is stocked with everything crew members need as they travel around the country. The hauler is 53 feet long and 13½ feet high, with a 150-gallon fuel tank on each side. When it's filled with equipment it weighs about 80,000 pounds (that's 40 tons). And it's no wonder Busch's big rig is so sweet — it's sponsored by M&M's!

Hot Wheels

The hauler holds the primary race car as well as a backup car in its top compartment, which is accessed by using a ladder and opening a hatch in the middle of the hauler. The backup remains on the transporter unless the primary car is wrecked before the race. The cars are loaded and unloaded using a mechanical-lift platform, which doubles as the back door of the trailer. It can lower a car in less than a minute.

On the Lookout

Once it arrives at a racetrack, the hauler converts into a command center. The observation deck is where crew chief Dave Rogers and the team's engineers keep an eye on the competition during practice and qualifying. Details about how fast each of the rival cars is going is recorded on a laptop and shared with the rest of the team before the race.

Tool Central

The inside of the transporter is lined with cabinets, drawers, and compartments. They contain tools and supplies such as springs, shocks, rotors, and transmissions – everything from tiny screws to a complete engine. "It has enough parts to build a car from the ground up," says Jellen. "We even have a drawer just for the decals on Kyle's car."

Getting in Gear

Team uniforms, helmets, and radios are stored in closets. Jellen makes sure that the firesuits for all 21 crew members are clean and that the headsets the team uses to communicate with Busch – and each other – during the race are charged and ready to go.

From Face-off To Tip-off

An inside look at the STAPLES Center's speedy changeover

This line is located dea[d] center of th[e] arena floor[.] Tip-off and[d] face-off happ[en] at the same exact spot.

The pieces that hold the Plexiglass in place are called stanchions.

3:49 P.M.

The Los Angeles Kings beat the Boston Bruins 4-3 in an exciting shootout. Because the game went into overtime, the STAPLES Center crew must hustle to get ready for an NBA game, which tips off in about four hours.

3:55 P.M.

The first order of business is to take down the Plexiglass around the rink. Forklifts help remove the Plexiglass and put them on racks.

3:59 P.M.

Next, the crew starts covering the ice with insulated plywood flooring. The overlay floor protects the rink's surface.

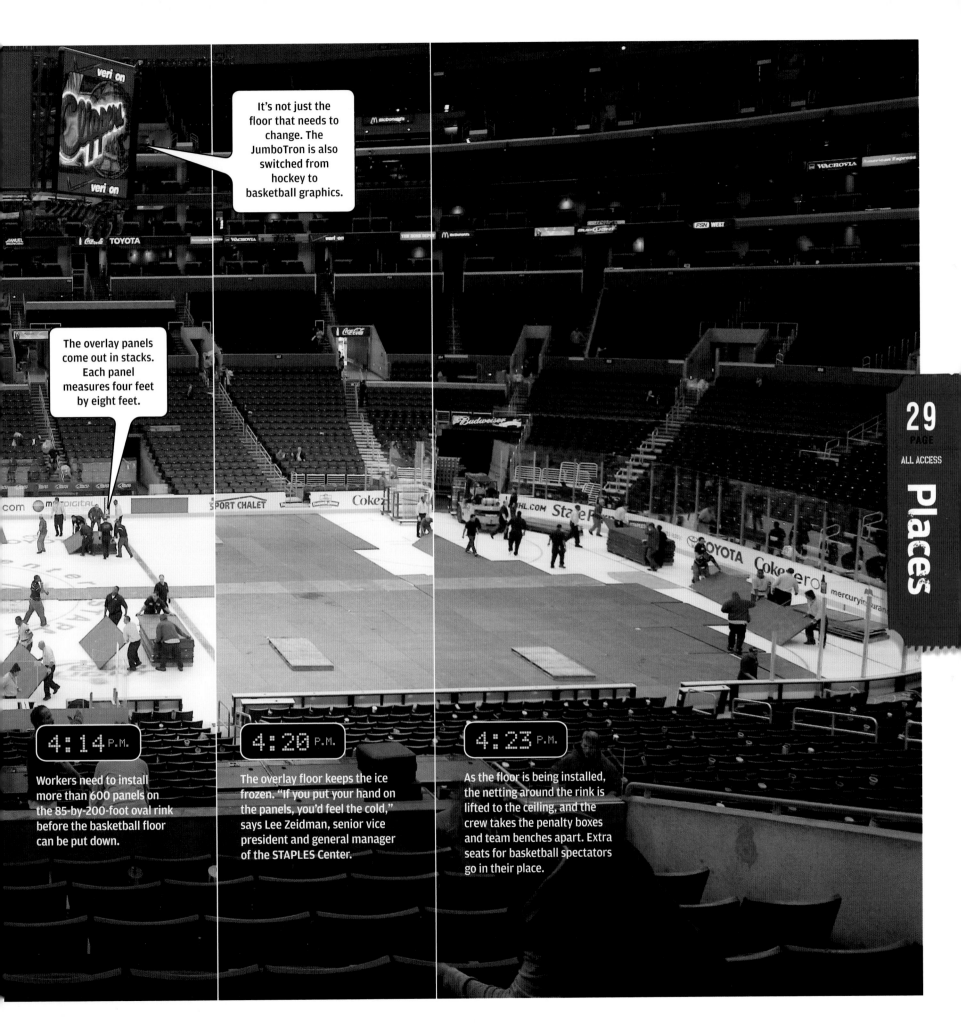

It's not just the floor that needs to change. The JumboTron is also switched from hockey to basketball graphics.

The overlay panels come out in stacks. Each panel measures four feet by eight feet.

4:14 P.M.

Workers need to install more than 600 panels on the 85-by-200-foot oval rink before the basketball floor can be put down.

4:20 P.M.

The overlay floor keeps the ice frozen. "If you put your hand on the panels, you'd feel the cold," says Lee Zeidman, senior vice president and general manager of the STAPLES Center.

4:23 P.M.

As the floor is being installed, the netting around the rink is lifted to the ceiling, and the crew takes the penalty boxes and team benches apart. Extra seats for basketball spectators go in their place.

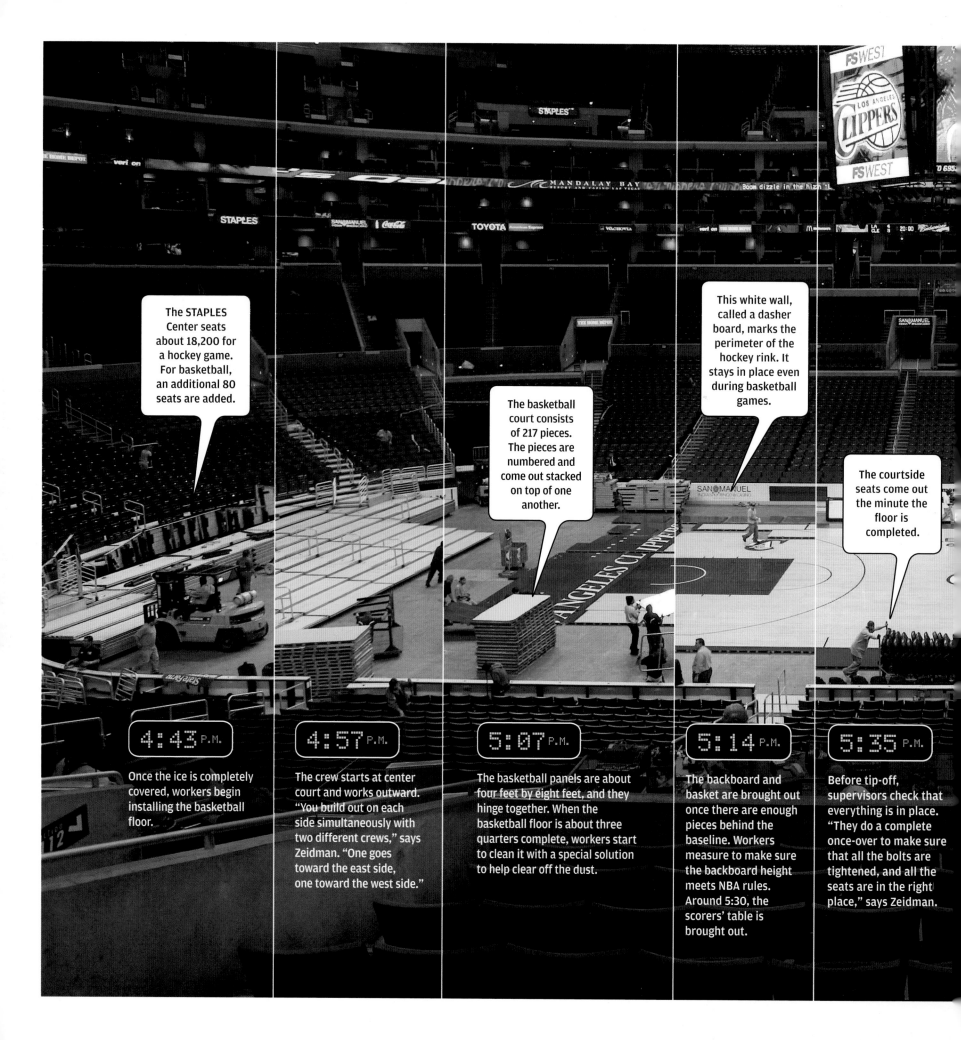

The STAPLES Center seats about 18,200 for a hockey game. For basketball, an additional 80 seats are added.

The basketball court consists of 217 pieces. The pieces are numbered and come out stacked on top of one another.

This white wall, called a dasher board, marks the perimeter of the hockey rink. It stays in place even during basketball games.

The courtside seats come out the minute the floor is completed.

4:43 P.M.

Once the ice is completely covered, workers begin installing the basketball floor.

4:57 P.M.

The crew starts at center court and works outward. "You build out on each side simultaneously with two different crews," says Zeidman. "One goes toward the east side, one toward the west side."

5:07 P.M.

The basketball panels are about four feet by eight feet, and they hinge together. When the basketball floor is about three quarters complete, workers start to clean it with a special solution to help clear off the dust.

5:14 P.M.

The backboard and basket are brought out once there are enough pieces behind the baseline. Workers measure to make sure the backboard height meets NBA rules. Around 5:30, the scorers' table is brought out.

5:35 P.M.

Before tip-off, supervisors check that everything is in place. "They do a complete once-over to make sure that all the bolts are tightened, and all the seats are in the right place," says Zeidman.

Tip-off!

icle of the NBA

7:44 P.M.

The Los Angeles Clippers tip off against the Cleveland Cavaliers in front of a packed house. The STAPLES Center crew completes the changeover about 200 times a year. It's no wonder these pros need only a few hours to transform an icy rink into a hardwood arena.

A Trip to Fantasyland

It's just another day at the office for skateboarder and reality TV star Rob Dyrdek

PLACE:	The Fantasy Factory
LOCATION:	Los Angeles, California
SIZE:	25,000 square feet

THE COOL STUFF:

- A skatepark that runs throughout the Factory and into the office space
- The world's biggest skateboard (more than 36-feet long)
- A tennis ball gun that fires balls up to 100 miles per hour
- A foam pit for practicing stunts

≪ Office Space

When he isn't playing in the Fantasy Factory, Dyrdek is busy hatching business ideas in his office. This custom chair was a birthday present from a skate shop in Virginia Beach, Virginia, and is built entirely out of Dyrdek's signature Alien Workshop skateboard decks.

⌃ For the Record

In 2009, Dyrdek set a Guinness World Record by building the world's largest skateboard. The board, which is more than 36-feet long and eight-feet wide, required a crane to move it to the center of the Factory. "That thing is basically like a runaway tractor trailer with no brakes," jokes Dyrdek. "I don't want to move it ever again."

⌃ Micro Machine

Of all the vehicles Dyrdek has accumulated in the Factory, his favorite is this miniature car. One-fifth the size of a real rally car, Dyrdek uses it to perform skids and tricks in the warehouse. He also drove the car in a highlight video with legendary rally car racer Ken Block. Block, piloting his full-sized rally car, and Dyrdek, navigating this tiny replica, drove side-by-side through a course performing stunts.

⌃ Zip It

When NBA stars like Carmelo Anthony, Ron Artest, and Lamar Odom visit, Dyrdek sends them to the Factory's main attraction: the zip line, which is accessible by climbing up to a tree house. It's not only fun, it might be the safest activity in the warehouse. "NBA dudes are just too big to [ride our BMX bikes]," says Dyrdek. "I don't want to be responsible for you [getting hurt and] losing your season."

≪ Under Attack

From his office, Dyrdek can climb a ladder through the ceiling to play with his tennis ball gun, a replica of the gadget on the old TV show *American Gladiators*. Dyrdek's receptionist, assistant, and manager are his favorite targets. The device can be put on wheels so that Dyrdek can go mobile and surprise his co-workers throughout the factory.

≪ Pit Stop

A giant ramp launches people into the foam pit. Rapper Ludacris once rode up the ramp on a motorcycle towing Dyrdek behind on a skateboard. When Dyrdek launched in the air, NBA star Carmelo Anthony passed him a basketball, which he shot through the hoop.

Toy Story ≫

Dyrdek created a toy line called Wild Grinders, based on his childhood skate crew. But working in the Fantasy Factory, you can't be too serious. "You can only work so much before you run down and mess around," says Dyrdek.

What Lurks Behind the Monster

Revealing the secrets behind Fenway Park's famous green wall

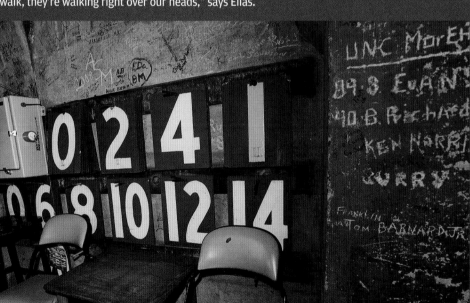

« Number Crunchers

The scorekeepers track the hits, runs, and errors during every home game. When a batter gets a hit or a runner scores, they put up a two-pound, 12-by-16 inch steel plate *(right)* in the appropriate spot to show the new tally. Runs are marked with a yellow number if a team is at bat, then switched to white at the end of each half-inning. The uniform numbers of the pitchers who are in the game *(left)* are also displayed.

⌄ Belly of the Beast

The scorekeepers' room has no bathroom, heat, or air conditioning. Because Fenway's foundation, made of reinforced steel and concrete, sinks 22 feet below the field, people must walk down a few steps to enter the Green Monster. "We're right below Lansdowne Street, so when fans are on the sidewalk, they're walking right over our heads," says Elias.

Pumped Up

Superstar athletes from all sports train at the University of Miami's state-of-the-art weight room

U CHAMPIONS ARE MADE

School Ties

How impressive is the Hurricane Strength and Conditioning Complex? Dozens of former Miami football players, including Baltimore Ravens safety Ed Reed and Washington Redskins wide receiver Santana Moss, return there to work out in the off-season under the watchful eye of strength and conditioning coach Andreu Swasey. And it's not just football players who use the facilities: New York Yankees third baseman Alex Rodriguez and Olympic sprinter Lauryn Williams have trained there too. Here are a few others.

Dwayne Johnson
Before he became "The Rock," Dwayne Johnson — who still drives 60 miles round-trip every day to work out in the Hurricanes' weight room — was a defensive tackle on Miami's 1991 national championship team. "The weight room is sacred," says Johnson. "It's important to me to always go back there."

Jonathan Vilma
New Orleans Saints linebacker Jonathan Vilma and tight end Jeremy Shockey, who won a national title together at Miami in 2001, worked out at their alma mater during the week leading up to Super Bowl XLIV. Then they played key roles as the Saints beat the Indianapolis Colts 31–17 in the big game.

Heavy Metal

The five-time national champion Hurricanes don't take their training lightly. The weight room, which was built for $4.5 million in 2001 and renovated in 2008, is at the top of its class. Besides the 22 tons of weights, the fitness complex also has stations for stretching and rehab. "It's nicer than my apartment," says Wayne. A typical incoming freshman football player at Miami increases his bench press and squat by 100 to 150 pounds, improves his vertical jump by five to seven inches, and takes .1 to .2 of a second off his 40-yard dash time by his senior season, according to Coach Swasey.

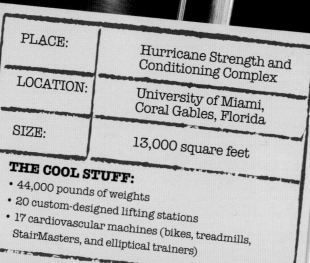

HURRICANE FOOTBALL ALL TIME RECORDS

PLAYER POSITION	BENCH PRESS	SQUAT	POWER CLEAN	40 YD DASH	20 YD SHUTTLE	VERTICAL JUMP
QB	R. COLLINS 405 '05	V. TESTAVERDE 500	K. FREEMAN 264 '07	K. KELLY 4.43	K. FREEMAN 4.08	R. KELLY 35"
RB	D. HARRIS 455 '95	D. HARRIS 655 '95	W. McGAHEE 360	W. McGAHEE 4.32 '02	J. JACKSON 4.00	W. McGAHEE 41.5"
WR	R. HILL 355 '90	J. POPOVITCH 500 '07	A. JOHNSON 320	S. SHIELDS 4.26	R. PARRISH 3.85 '03	S. MOSS 42"
TE	C. HENRY 400 '07	D. FARR 555 '05	G. OLSEN 362	K. WILLIAMS 4.45	K. WINSLOW 4.06	D. EPPS 37" '07
OT	V. CAREY 480 '03	K. BLAISE 620	E. WINSTON 360 '06	E. WINSTON 4.78 '03	E. WINSTON 4.33 '03	T. BYRD 34.5"
G-C	C. CALLEJAS 500 '07	A. BAIN 650	T. WISE 360	D. HANDY 4.76	C. MYERS 4.25 '03	M. BIRLA 32"
K-P	M. BOSHER 315	M. BOSHER 450 '07	M. BOSHER 301 '07	B. MONROE 4.62	R. MONROE 3.92	B. MONROE 36"
DT	D. SILEO 535 '85	J. BURT 680 '85	M. LAWSON 320	M. LAWSON 4.71	M. LAWSON 4.34	R. STINSON 33.5"
DE	K. FAGEN 560 '05	D. FORTNEY 555 '07	A. BAILEY 375	K. HARRIS 4.46	R. HOLMES 4.25	A. BAILEY 38" '07
LB	D. MIRA 455 '07	V. MORRIS 600 '05	D.J. WILLIAMS 360	J. WEAVER 4.35	C. CAMPBELL 3.90	C. WILSON 42"
CB	L. MYERS 375 '95	A. ROLLE 445	A. ROLLE 313	M. MAXEY 4.25	P. BUCHANON 3.88	D. SHARPE 41.5"
S	A. MOSER 350 '06	R. PHILLIPS 500 '07	S. TAYLOR 313	D. WILLIAMS 4.34	A. MOSER 3.85	R. PHILLIPS 40"

Weighty Matters

Miami's strength and conditioning board lists the Hurricanes' alltime records in the weight room and in speed and conditioning drills, broken down by position. Former Hurricanes quarterback Vinny Testaverde still holds the QB squat mark (a hefty 500 pounds) and is the only player who has been on the board since it was created in 1985. Through 2009, former running back Willis McGahee, kicker Matt Bosher, punter Brian Monroe, and offensive tackle Eric Winston were tied for the most records, with three apiece.

Reggie Wayne

Indianapolis Colts wide receiver Reggie Wayne, who led the NFL in receiving yards in 2007 and was named to his fourth straight Pro Bowl in 2009, credits part of his success to his off-season work in Miami's weight room. "It's like our own fraternity," says Wayne.

PLACE:	Hurricane Strength and Conditioning Complex
LOCATION:	University of Miami, Coral Gables, Florida
SIZE:	13,000 square feet

THE COOL STUFF:
- 44,000 pounds of weights
- 20 custom-designed lifting stations
- 17 cardiovascular machines (bikes, treadmills, StairMasters, and elliptical trainers)

PLACE:	Dallas Mavericks Locker Room
LOCATION:	American Airlines Center, Dallas, Texas
SIZE:	8,000 square feet

THE COOL STUFF:
- Each player's locker includes a built-in 19-inch HDTV with satellite TV connection
- Personal MP3/stereo systems and customized $400 headphones
- Personal DVD players and PlayStation 3s

Home Sweet Home

Dirk Nowitzki gives us the scoop on Dallas's fancy locker room

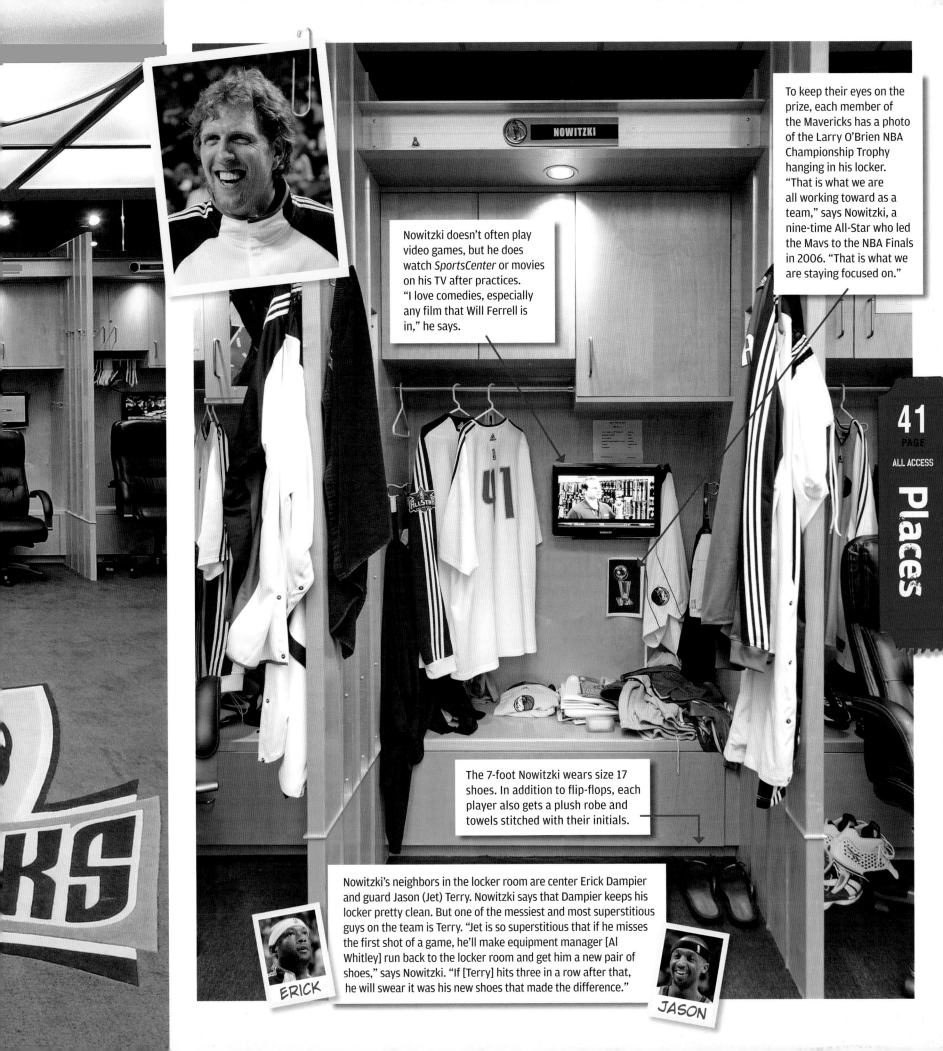

NOWITZKI

To keep their eyes on the prize, each member of the Mavericks has a photo of the Larry O'Brien NBA Championship Trophy hanging in his locker. "That is what we are all working toward as a team," says Nowitzki, a nine-time All-Star who led the Mavs to the NBA Finals in 2006. "That is what we are staying focused on."

Nowitzki doesn't often play video games, but he does watch *SportsCenter* or movies on his TV after practices. "I love comedies, especially any film that Will Ferrell is in," he says.

The 7-foot Nowitzki wears size 17 shoes. In addition to flip-flops, each player also gets a plush robe and towels stitched with their initials.

Nowitzki's neighbors in the locker room are center Erick Dampier and guard Jason (Jet) Terry. Nowitzki says that Dampier keeps his locker pretty clean. But one of the messiest and most superstitious guys on the team is Terry. "Jet is so superstitious that if he misses the first shot of a game, he'll make equipment manager [Al Whitley] run back to the locker room and get him a new pair of shoes," says Nowitzki. "If [Terry] hits three in a row after that, he will swear it was his new shoes that made the difference."

ERICK

JASON

>> INSIDE ALL THE COOL STUFF THAT HELPS ATHLETES DO THEIR JOBS

Gear

Suit of Armor

A look at the protection underneath an NFL player's uniform

HELMET
Daniels still uses the same model Riddell helmet that he wore at Naperville (Illinois) Central High School and at the University of Wisconsin.

SHOULDER PADS
Daniels's shoulder pads protect his shoulders, chest, and ribs during all the pushing, tackles, and pileups that occur during a game. The pads are made of a hard plastic shell that goes on top of foam padding. They are secured with snaps and buckles. Daniels also uses a trick of the trade, sticking double-sided tape on his pads so that his jersey sticks to them. "That way it's not loose and people can't grab me as easily," he says.

GLOVES
Through the 2009 season, Daniels ranked second alltime on the Texans in receptions (207) and receiving yards (2,501). So it's not surprising that his favorite pieces of equipment are his gloves. "I get a fresh pair for each game, and sometimes even change them out at halftime," he says. "When you get them right out of the package, they're pretty sticky and the ball won't slip through." The gloves also protect his hands when he blocks for teammates.

THIGH PADS
Unlike many of his fellow pass catchers, Daniels wears thigh pads, which are made of lightweight foam and mold to the body. "Receivers tend to not wear them because their game is all about speed, and they don't usually get hit unless they have the ball in their hands," he says. "But I get banged around a lot while I'm blocking people, so I have to protect my thighs and my knees."

SHOES
Daniels likes his footwear simple and sleek. "The lighter the better," he says of his size-13 cleats, which help him grip the field without slipping. "One of my biggest assets is having quickness when I run my routes. So every little ounce helps." But style counts too. "The shoes have to look good," says Daniels, who goes through about five pairs a season. His newest model, the Nike Speed TD cleat, features a mirrored, reflective bottom. "That way when you're running away after a reception people will notice you," he says with a laugh.

Evolution of Shoulder Pads

From flimsy padding sewn into shirts to the hard plastic and foam players wear today

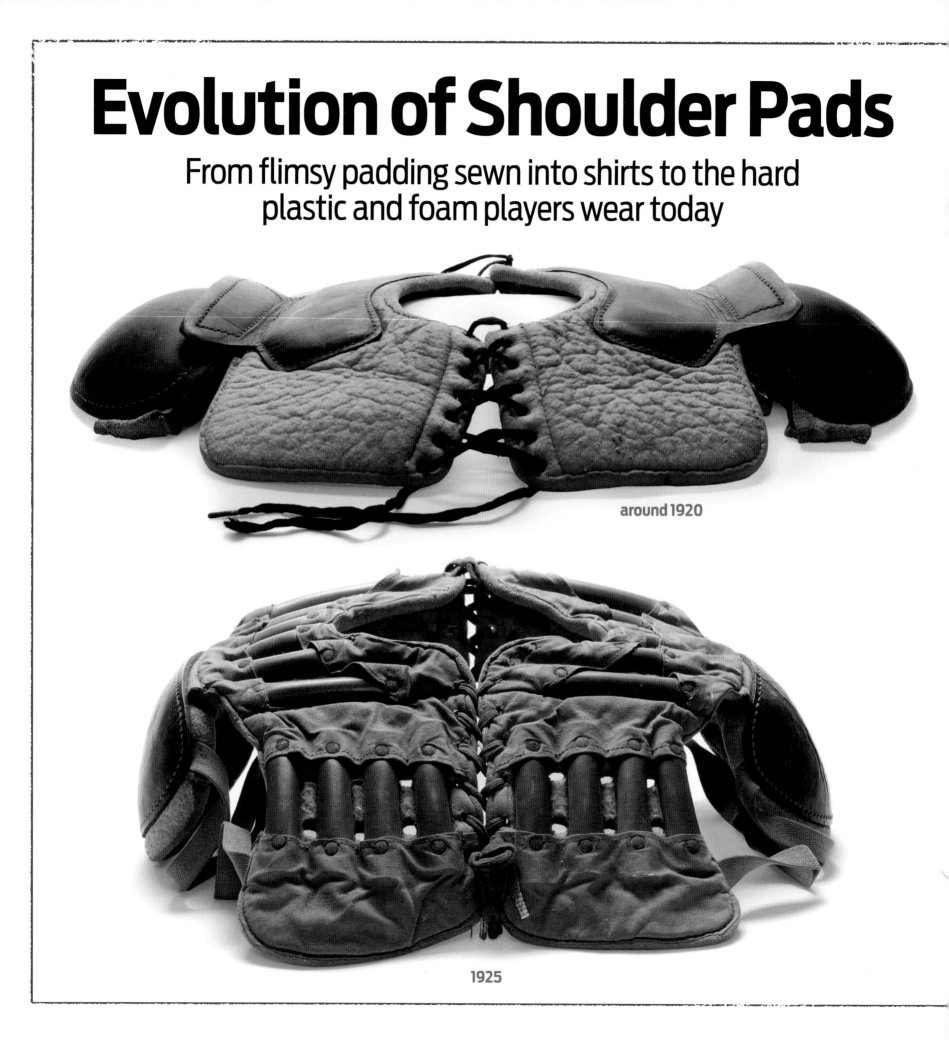

around 1920

1925

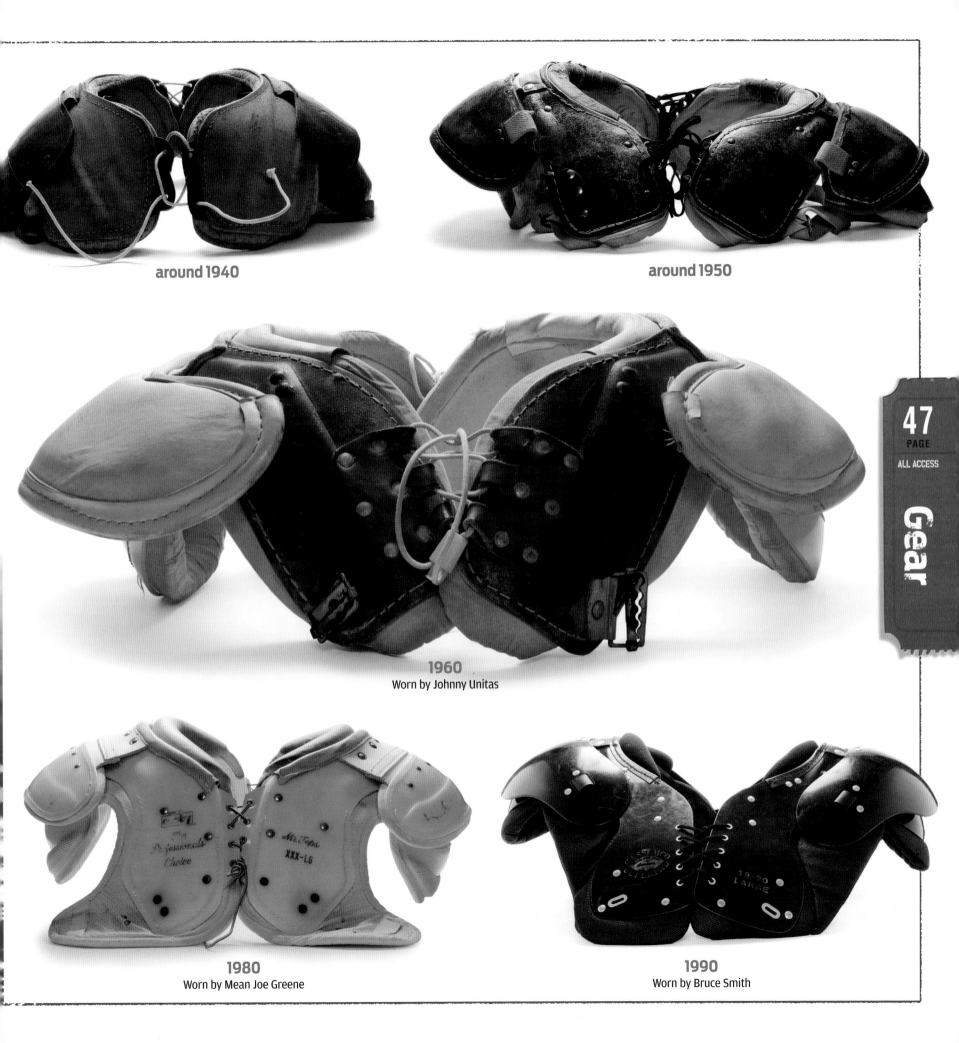

around 1940

around 1950

1960
Worn by Johnny Unitas

1980
Worn by Mean Joe Greene

1990
Worn by Bruce Smith

Behind the Mask

The Buffalo Sabres' Ryan Miller explains the detailed artwork on his goalie helmet

The Puck Stops Here
One of the NHL's top goalies, Miller also led Team USA to an Olympic silver medal in 2010.

More Tales of the Mask

JOHAN HEDBERG
Atlanta Thrashers

In 2001, Hedberg was called up by the Pittsburgh Penguins from the Manitoba Moose, a minor league team in Canada. He didn't have time to alter his mask, which featured his former team's mascot, so people in Pittsburgh took to cheering "Mooooooose!" every time Hedberg made a save. The nickname stuck. "At first I didn't like it," says Hedberg, "because it didn't seem personal. But it caught on with the fans. And over the years the moose has become a good-luck charm."

Moose on the Loose

Hedberg has sported a moose for his entire career. He and artist David Gunnarsson have created more than eight versions of Max Moosy, a cartoon character. Max has appeared on Hedberg's mask as Indiana Moose, an ode to the movie *Raiders of the Lost Ark*, and as SpongeMoose SquarePants, which was inspired by Hedberg's daughter. "She's a big fan of the SpongeBob show, and I like it too," he says.

Team Spirit

When his mask broke after being hit by a puck during a game in 2009, Hedberg and Gunnarsson created a new model. "We decided to downplay the moose a little in favor of emphasizing the team," says Hedberg. The Thrashers' logo is more prominently displayed and Gunnarsson also airbrushed smaller versions into the royal-blue paint on each side.

DAN ELLIS
Nashville Predators

Ellis took an active role in designing his mask, which also was created by artist David Gunnarsson. "I was into art as a kid, so I can draw fairly well," says Ellis, whose mask features two saber-toothed tigers modeled after Nashville's mascot. "I think every goalie has a special connection to his mask," he says. "It's our way of expressing our identity while we're on the ice."

Color Coordinated
The mask was designed specifically to match Nashville's third jersey, which the players wear during Saturday-night home games. Like the jerseys, the mask has a black-and-blue checkered pattern.

Ferocious
The tigers on both sides of the mask have exposed rib bones as a result of being in a tough battle. "They represent drive and determination," says Ellis. "I wanted to show that I was hungry and ready to compete for the starting [goalie] spot this year."

Chin Music
On the chin, Ellis's number 39 is painted in the same style as the logo of his favorite band, Nickelback.

CAM WARD
Carolina Hurricanes

Cam Ward carries his helmets in a special case. "I tend to baby my masks," says Ward, whose junior hockey coach didn't allow painted masks. "I had an all-black one until I turned pro at age 21. That's why I'm so excited about getting creative with my masks now." Artist Steve Nash of EYECANDYAIR airbrushes the designs on Ward's mask with paint, then locks in the artwork with four layers of clear coat "so it can stand up to those 100-mile-per-hour pucks," says Nash.

Pirate Attack
Ward, who won the Stanley Cup as a rookie in 2006, chose a pirate theme for his mask because Blackbeard, a famous 18th-century buccaneer, sailed along the coast of North Carolina. The mask shows the swashbuckler holding a hockey stick and lunging over the Hurricanes' logo. Ward liked how the image "related to both the state and to the team."

Personal Touch
The bottom of the mask features Ward's nickname, Wardo, in Old English script. His number, 30, is incorporated into the swirls above his forehead. "Cam wanted the number to appear windblown," says Nash, "like it was being pounded by a hurricane."

STEVE MASON
Columbus Blue Jackets

Steve Mason grew up in Canada, but his mask pays tribute to his adopted home. "It's dedicated to Columbus, Ohio," says Mason, the 2008–09 NHL rookie of the year. "I wanted to show some of the city's landmarks and history."

His new mask was custom-molded to fit his head. Mason had to have his entire face wrapped in a cast. "It was uncomfortable having that goop all over my head for 20 minutes," says Mason. But now the helmet "fits like a second skin," he says.

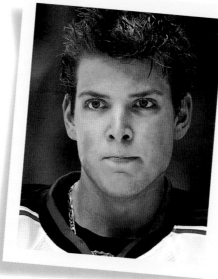

State Pride
In addition to an outline of the state and a sketch of Christopher Columbus's ship, the *Santa Maria*, on the right side of the mask, the bottom is wrapped in Ohio's red, white and blue state flag.

Lock Down
The Blue Jackets' home rink, Nationwide Arena, was built on the former site of the Ohio State Penitentiary. A sketch of the prison, which some fans believed gave the team bad luck, appears on the left side of Mason's mask. The netminder helped put that curse to rest in 2008-09 when he led the Blue Jackets to the playoffs for the first time in team history.

In the Driver's Seat
On the chin, Mason's nickname, Mase, appears in the style of an Ohio license plate.

Playing Hardball

We peel back the layers of a baseball

Third winding

Fourth winding

Second winding

First winding

SPIN A YARN
The first of four windings is made of gray woolen yarn. If you were to stretch out all the yarn in just this first layer, it would measure 121 yards.

HEART OF THE MATTER
The core of a baseball is a small ball made from cork and rubber.

MORE FLUFF
A final layer of white polyester-cotton yarn is wound around two more woolen-yarn layers for a total of four windings. All together more than 300 yards of yarn are used, giving the baseball a diameter of 8.86 inches.

RUBBER BAND
The center ball is surrounded by two layers of rubber, one black and one red. This section is called the pill.

Wood Stock

Every Louisville Slugger starts life as a log at one of three mills owned by Larimer & Norton. Logs typically come from trees that are between 50 and 80 years old. A single tree can produce about 35 to 40 bats. The company is constantly growing new trees to replace the old ones.

⌄ Making the Cut

The logs start out 10 to 14 feet long. Inside the mill, they are stripped of bark and cut into 40-inch-long sections. Smaller tubes, called billets, are then cut out of each log. All billets come from the area near the outside edge of the log, where the wood is newer and stronger.

And Then There's the Bat...

A Louisville Slugger's journey from big trees to the big leagues

Grading System ≫

Wood is graded based on the grain. The best bats have straight grains that are widely and evenly spaced, like the one at the far right. Once the billets arrive at the Louisville Slugger factory, they are graded again. The best billets are turned into bats for major league players. Billets that are just a grade below the top are turned into the bats you buy at the store.

≪ Mean Machine

Each major league team's equipment manager sends an order to Louisville Slugger. Players specify their choice of wood (ash or maple), bat shape, length, weight, color, finish, and signature type. A Computer Numerical Control (CNC) machine then shapes the billet into the correct bat model. This CNC Machine is making Derek Jeter's P72 bat.

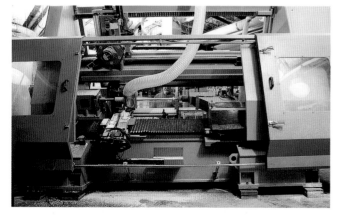

❮❮ Taking Shape

Special saws produce 18 to 20 high-quality billets from each log. After the billets are cut, they are ready to be graded.

Good Wood ❯❯

Billets are stamped with their weight in ounces. Because the wood is damp, the billets spend four to five weeks drying in a kiln. They are covered in wax to prevent cracking and cut down to 37 inches. Then they are graded and shipped to the Louisville Slugger factory in Kentucky.

GENUINE P72
New York Yankees

❮ Serious Heat

Players can specify whether they'd like their name, signature, and the company logo burned onto the bat, or stamped on with oil dyes.

Sign Here❯❯

Signatures are burned on with 1,400-degree brand. There is a metal autograph stamp of every player who has ever signed on with the company, going back to guys like Babe Ruth and Hank Aaron.

❮❮ Final Touches

Separate machines sand the bat and remove the knobs at the top and bottom, which had been used to hold the bat in place in various machines. Some bats have part of the end drilled out to make them lighter.

⌃ Paint Job

Colored bats are dipped in paint, then hung to dry. A worker uses a sponge to dab the drips off the end of the bat. Once the bat is no longer dripping, it is dried for about 15 minutes using UV light.

Gear

❮❮ Ready for Action!

Derek Jeter uses a black bat with his signature stamped on. Once the paint has dried, it's ready to be shipped to Yankee Stadium. An everyday player like Jeter will go through about 100 bats each season. Jeter's custom-made lumber has helped him get almost 3,000 hits in his career.

PHOTO CREDITS

Cover: Heinz Kluetmeier (Mets clubhouse, 2); *Inside Cover:* Dave Reginek/NHLI/Getty Images (Red Wings dressing room) *Title Page:* Heinz Kluetmeier (Green Monster door) *Contents:* Al Tielemans (bats) *Pages 4-7:* Heinz Kluetmeier (O'Neal portrait); Greg Nelson (hands and palm); John Biever (O'Neal action); Todd Rosenberg (Johnson hand); Al Tielemans (Johnson action) *Pages 8-11:* Andrew Hancock (Sims, turtle, tarantula); Getty Images/National Geographic (kinkajou); Steve Barrett (Shiancoe); Rich Frishman (Deneen); Darren Carroll (Ohlendorf) *Pages 12-13:* Jason Wise (Hill) *Pages 14-15:* Erik Isakson (Teter) *Pages 16-19:* Layne Murdoch/NBAE/Getty Images (Paul); Courtesy of Jordan Brand (sneakers) *Pages 20-23:* Heinz Kluetmeier (Mets clubhouse, 10) *Pages 24-27:* Todd Bigelow/Aurora (Busch portrait); Michael J. LeBrecht II/1Deuce3 Photography (hauler); Illustration by Don Foley *Pages 28-31:* John W. McDonough (STAPLES Center, 12; Fantasy Factory, 8) *Pages 32-37:* Damian Strohmeyer (action, 2); Heinz Kluetmeier (Green Monster, 7) *Pages 38-39:* Bill Frakes (weight room, 3); Marcel Thomas/FilmMagic (Johnson); Chris Graythen/Getty Images (Vilma); Rob Tringali/Sportschrome/Getty Images (Wayne) *Pages 40-41:* Greg Nelson (Mavericks locker room, Nowitzki locker, Nowitzki, Dampier); Garrett W. Ellwood/NBAE/Getty Images (Terry) *Pages 42-47:* Greg Nelson (Daniels, 2); Courtesy of Pro Football Hall of Fame (shoulder pads, 7) *Pages 48-55:* Bill Wippert/NHLI/Getty Images (Miller action); Al Tielemans (Miller portrait, front of mask, back of mask); Jeff Vinnick/NHLI/Getty Images (Hedberg headshot); Scott Cunningham (Hedberg mask, 3); Eliot J. Schechter/NHLI/Getty Images (Ellis headshot); John Russell (Ellis mask, 3); Len Redkoles/NHLI/Getty Images (Ward headshot); Scott Pilling (Ward mask, 3); Jeff Gross/Getty Images (Mason headshot); Jamie Sabau (Mason mask, 3) *Pages 56-59:* Brad Mangin (Lincecum); Peter Gregoire (ball, 3) *Pages 60-61:* Al Tielemans (making of the bat, 10); Steven Freeman (Jeter's bat); Gregory Heisler (Jeter portrait) *Copyright Page:* Nathaniel S. Butler/NBAE/Getty Images (James) *Back Inside Cover:* G. Newman Lowrance/Getty Images (Rams locker room) *Back Cover:* John W. McDonough (Dyrdek); Heinz Kluetmeier (Green Monster); Greg Nelson (Mavericks locker room)

TIME HOME ENTERTAINMENT

Publisher . . . . Richard Fraiman
General Manager . . . . Steven Sandonato
Executive Director, Marketing Services . . . . Carol Pittard
Director, Retail & Special Sales . . . . Tom Mifsud
Director, New Product Development . . . . Peter Harper
Director, Bookazine Development & Marketing . . . . Laura Adam
Publishing Director, Brand Marketing . . . . Joy Butts
Assistant General Counsel . . . . Helen Wan
Brand & Licensing Manager . . . . Alexandra Bliss
Design & Prepress Manager . . . . Anne-Michelle Gallero
Book Production Manager . . . . Susan Chodakiewicz
Associate Brand Manager . . . . Allison Parker

SPECIAL THANKS: Christine Austin, Jeremy Biloon, Glenn Buonocore, Jim Childs, Rose Cirrincione, Jacqueline Fitzgerald, Carrie Frazier, Lauren Hall, Jennifer Jacobs, Suzanne Janso, Brynn Joyce, Mona Li, Robert Marasco, Amy Migliaccio, Kimberly Posa, Brooke Reger, Dave Rozzelle, Ilene Schreider, Adriana Tierno, Alex Voznesenskiy, Sydney Webber

ISBN 10: 1-60320-154-8
ISBN 13: 978-1-60320-154-4
Library of Congress Control Number: 2010923766

Sports Illustrated Kids is a trademark of Time Inc.

We welcome your comments and suggestions about Sports Illustrated Kids Books. Please write to us at: Sports Illustrated Kids Books, Attention: Book Editors, PO Box 11016, Des Moines, IA 50336-1016

If you would like to order any of our hardcover Collector's Edition books, please call us at 1-800-327-6388. (Monday through Friday, 7:00 a.m.– 8:00 p.m. or Saturday, 7:00 a.m.– 6:00 p.m. Central Time).

Alone Time
Cleveland Cavaliers forward LeBron James enjoys a quiet moment before a game.

Cram Session
The visiting St. Louis Rams handle last-minute preparations in the visitors' locker room at Soldier Field before taking on the Chicago Bears